Aberdeenshire
COUNCIL

Aberdeenshire Library and Information Service
www.aberdeenshire.gov.uk/libraries
Renewals Hotline 01224 661511

First published 2009
Evans Brothers Limited
2A Portman Mansions
Chiltern Street
London W1U 6NR

British Library Cataloguing in Publication Data

Gowar, Mick, 1951-
    Tuva. -- (Spirals)
    1. Children's stories.
    I. Title II. Series
    823.9'14-dc22

ISBN: 978 0 237 53879 8 (hb)
ISBN: 978 0 237 53885 9 (pb)

Printed in China

Editor: Louise John
Design: Robert Walster
Production: Jenny Mulvanny

Tuva

Mick Gowar
and Tone Eriksen

Evans

I'm Tuva the puppy.
I bark and I fight.
I sing to the moon
through the long summer night.

I'm Tuva the hardy.
I'm brave and I'm bold –
I laugh at the blizzard,
I sneer at the cold.

I need no warm house
when storm winds blow.
I scrape out a hollow,
I sleep in the snow.

When I'm put in my harness,
I listen and learn.
I know when to stop,
and I know when to turn.

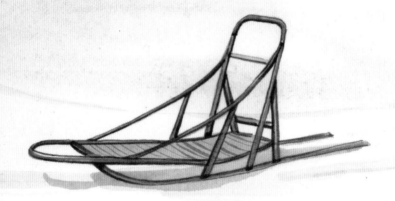

I'm Tuva the sledge dog,
I'm tough and I'm strong.
I can pull a packed sledge
through snow all day long.

Across oceans of whiteness,
my dog team and me.
To where mountains of ice
tumble into the sea.

And above the great water,
in the pink evening sky,
the ghostly green dancers
are twirling on high.

I'm Tuva the lead dog.
I'm boss of the team.
I'm faithful and tireless.
I'm tough and I'm keen.

I'm Tuva the mighty –
you wolves best beware.
I once won a fight
with a great polar bear.

We were out on the ice,
as the morning mist cleared,
when out of the water
the monster appeared.

He was two metres tall,
with long vicious claws,
that gleamed like steel hooks
on the ends of his paws.

His teeth were like knives,
and he roared in his might –
but I was the braver
and put him to flight.

I'm Tuva the faithful.
Of my pack I'm the last.
I guard Master's door.
No danger gets past.

I'm Tuva the old dog,
my master's best friend.
I sleep by his side
when the day's at an end.

31

Why not try reading another **Spirals** book?

Megan's Tick Tock Rocket by Andrew Fusek Peters, Polly Peters
HB: 978 0237 53348 0 PB: 978 0237 53342 7

Growl! by Vivian French
HB: 978 0237 53351 0 PB: 978 0237 53345 8

John and the River Monster by Paul Harrison
HB: 978 0237 53350 2 PB: 978 0237 53344 1

Froggy Went a Hopping by Alan Durant
HB: 978 0237 53352 9 PB: 978 0237 53346 5

Amy's Slippers by Mary Chapman
HB: 978 0237 53353 3 PB: 978 0237 53347 2

The Flamingo Who Forgot by Alan Durant
HB: 978 0237 53349 6 PB: 978 0237 53343 4

Glub! by Penny Little
HB: 978 0237 53462 2 PB: 978 0237 53461 5

The Grumpy Queen by Valerie Wilding
HB: 978 0237 53460 8 PB: 978 0237 53459 2

Happy by Mara Bergman
HB: 978 0237 53532 2 PB: 978 0237 53536 0

Sink or Swim by Dereen Taylor
HB: 978 0237 53531 5 PB: 978 0237 53535 3

Sophie's Timepiece by Mary Chapman
HB: 978 0237 53530 8 PB: 978 0237 53534 6

The Perfect Prince by Paul Harrison
HB: 978 0237 53533 9 PB: 978 0237 53537 7

Tuva by Mick Gowar
HB: 978 0237 53879 8 PB: 978 0237 53885 9

Wait a Minute, Ruby! by Mary Chapman
HB: 978 0237 53882 8 PB: 978 0237 53888 0

George and the Dragonfly by Andy Blackford
HB: 978 0237 53878 1 PB: 978 0237 53884 2

Monster in the Garden by Anne Rooney
HB: 978 0237 53883 5 PB: 978 0237 53889 7

Just Custard by Joe Hackett
HB: 978 0237 53881 1 PB: 978 0237 53887 3

The King of Kites by Judith Heneghan
HB: 978 0237 53880 4 PB: 978 0237 53886 6